The
Firebird

Retold by Mairi Mackinnon

Illustrated by Alida Massari

Reading consultant: Alison Kelly
Roehampton University

Contents

Chapter 1

The apple thief

Long ago and far away, there lived a rich and powerful king. He had a magnificent palace, surrounded by beautiful gardens, but his greatest treasure was a magical orchard.

The trees in this orchard had gold and silver trunks and emerald leaves, and they blossomed with diamonds and rubies. When the sun shone, they sparkled and flashed like fireworks and, when the wind blew, they jingled like tiny bells.

Right in the middle was the most precious tree of all. Every year, its branches were weighed down with a crop of solid golden apples.

The orchard was surrounded by a high wall with a locked gate, and guarded day and night.

So the king was astonished to see, one September morning, that one golden apple was missing.

He sent for the guards at once, but they had seen nothing. He doubled the guard, but the next day another apple had been taken, and the day after, yet another.

The king had three brave sons, and they were determined to catch the thief. The eldest, Prince Dimitri, went out with the guards the very next night, and took up his post under the apple tree.

All night he stood and waited, but there was no sign of the thief. At last, the sky began to grow pale before sunrise. Disappointed, Prince Dimitri sat down under the tree to rest his aching body, and closed his eyes.

Moments later, he woke with
a start. Another apple had been
stolen, and the thief hadn't left so
much as a footprint in the dewy
grass. Once again, the guards had
seen nothing.

The following night, Prince Vassily was determined to do better. He patrolled the orchard all night long, and called the guards together at least every hour.

Just before daybreak, the guards failed to answer his call.

The prince went to find them, and was horrified to see that they were fast asleep. He woke them angrily and rushed back to the tree, but it was too late. The thief had been and gone.

Prince Ivan took his turn the next night, although his brothers were certain he wouldn't succeed.

"The thief must be a powerful magician," they said. "He casts a spell that no one can resist."

Prince Ivan shrugged, and went to wait under the apple tree.

As morning drew near, he felt unbearably sleepy, so he walked around the tree and sang songs to keep himself awake. The sky grew so bright, he thought the sun must be rising already. But it wasn't the sun...

13

To his astonishment,
Prince Ivan saw a
beautiful bird. Its body
glowed like burning coals, and its
long wing and tail feathers fluttered
like flames. The firebird circled the
orchard, then swooped down and
snatched an apple in its long beak.

14

Ivan leaped up and caught the
bird, but its body was so scorching
hot that he let it go again. He
was left with only a single bright
feather from its tail.

The king could hardly believe it
when Ivan brought him the feather
and told his story. "I must have
that bird!" he declared.

"I will find it for you, Father," said
Prince Dimitri at once. He saddled
his horse and set out immediately.

A month later, he came trudging
back, empty-handed and frustrated.

"Father, let me go," pleaded Prince Vassily. A month later he, too, came back without the bird.

"You'll never find it," the brothers told Ivan. "We've searched the entire kingdom. No one has ever seen a firebird – if it even exists."

Chapter 2

The wolf in the forest

Prince Ivan didn't let his brothers stop him. Taking the Firebird's feather, he rode off, deep into a winter forest.

Snow covered the ground and weighed down the branches of the trees. It muffled all sounds except his horse's careful footprints. The air was bitterly cold, but the Firebird's feather glowed brightly, keeping Ivan warm.

After a while, Ivan came to a crossroads with a faded signpost. Peering up at it, he read the signs.

FAILURE

WOLVES WILL DEVOUR YOU

WOLVES WILL EAT YOUR HORSE

HUNGER AND COLD

"Surely I can fight off a few wolves," thought Ivan, turning left. But for the first time ever, his horse refused to obey him, and galloped off to the right.

Almost at once, a great silver wolf sprang out of the forest and attacked them.

Ivan drove the beast away with his sword, but it was too late. His horse had chosen to die in order to save him. He broke down and cried.

Suddenly, he sensed that he was being watched. He looked up to see the same silver wolf, its head bowed in shame.

"I couldn't help myself," the wolf murmured. "I was so hungry. What can I do to make it up to you?"

"What can *you* do?" asked Ivan angrily. "What can *I* do? How am I supposed to find the Firebird without even a horse to ride?"

"Well, you could ride on my back," offered Silver Wolf. "I will take you to King Dalmat's palace. You will find the Firebird there."

Chapter 3

The Firebird and the Horse of Power

Nervously, Prince Ivan climbed onto Silver Wolf's back. The wolf sprang up, cleared the trees and flew through the winter air.

They soared over snowy woods, fields and villages, until night fell. At last, they saw the lights of a great palace in the distance.

"That is King Dalmat's palace," said Silver Wolf. "If you climb to the top of the tallest tower, you will find the Firebird in a golden cage. Take the Firebird but, whatever you do, don't touch her cage."

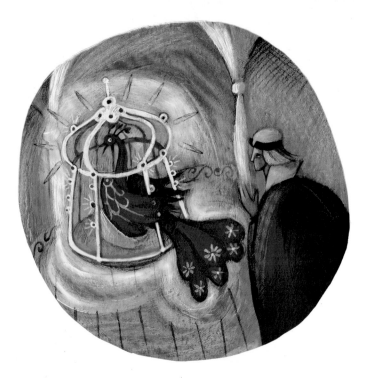

Ivan crept through the palace gardens and found the tower door unlocked. Silently, he climbed the stairs. There at the top was the Firebird, just as the wolf had promised. She fluttered around a golden cage that glittered with precious stones.

"How can I carry her without a cage?" Ivan wondered. "She'll burn me if I even touch her." He picked up the cage, and bells and alarms instantly rang through the palace. Guards rushed in, and dragged Ivan off to the palace prison.

The next morning he was brought
before King Dalmat, who looked at
him curiously.

"What kind of a prince acts like
a common thief?" he wondered.

Ivan told him the story of his
father's orchard, the Firebird and
his meeting with Silver Wolf. Then
he showed him the glowing feather.

"You're a brave young man," said King Dalmat at last. "I will give you the Firebird – if you will do something for me. Many years ago, King Afron stole my Horse of Power. Bring her back, and the Firebird is yours."

"Take her feather with you," he added. "One day it may help you more than you can imagine."

Ivan left the palace, and found
Silver Wolf waiting in the woods
nearby. The wolf seemed to know
exactly what he was going to say.

"King Afron's palace, is it?" he
asked. "Climb on, then." He leaped
above the trees.

They soared over high mountains and icy oceans, until night fell. At last, they saw the lights of another great palace.

"Look, there are the stables," said the wolf. "You'll find the Horse of Power in the very last stall. Bring the horse but, whatever you do, don't touch her bridle."

Ivan crept across the palace
courtyard and found the stable
door unlocked. There in the last
stall was the Horse of Power, just
as the wolf had promised. She
had a pearly-white coat, golden
wings and a golden mane and tail.
On the wall was a golden bridle,
covered with precious stones.

Ivan remembered the wolf's words. "But how can I lead her out of the stable without a bridle?" he wondered. He tried to take down another, but his sleeve brushed the golden one.

Bells and alarms rang out, even louder than before. Guards rushed in, and dragged Ivan off to prison.

The next morning he was
brought before King Afron,
who looked at him curiously.
"What kind of a prince
steals horses in the night?"
he wondered.

Ivan told him the story of his
father's orchard, the Firebird,
Silver Wolf and King Dalmat.

King Afron put his head in his
hands. "I wish I had your youth
and your courage," he said. "I will
gladly give you the Horse of Power,
if you will do something for me."

"Many years ago, the demon
Koshchey stole my only daughter.
I know that he keeps her prisoner
in his castle, but he is a very
powerful sorcerer, and I have never
been able to set her free. Bring
back my daughter, and you shall
have the horse with my blessing."

Chapter 4

Koshchey the Deathless

Prince Ivan left the palace, and found Silver Wolf in a ruined house nearby. For the first time, the wolf looked anxious.

"Koshchey's castle, is it?" he asked. "You'll need all your strength and courage there. Climb on."

Silver Wolf leaped into the sky, and they soared over teeming cities and dusty deserts. Finally, in the evening light, they saw the high, dark walls of a castle.

They landed on a mountain crag,
and watched the castle from a knot
of fir trees. "We must wait until
Koshchey is asleep," Silver Wolf
advised. "He will know we are here
soon enough."

After a while, Silver Wolf said "Now!" They leaped over the castle wall, and landed in a garden filled with rose trees and statues. Twelve beautiful girls were dancing around a fountain and laughing.

Startled to see Ivan, they stopped, and a gentle voice called, "What is it? What's the matter?"

A princess came into the garden, even more beautiful than the girls. For a moment she looked overjoyed to see Ivan, then frightened.

"Go, quickly!" she insisted. "If Koshchey finds you, he will turn you to stone, just like the others."

Ivan looked more closely at the statues. With horror, he saw that they were all knights and princes. Many had their swords raised, stone-frozen in rage and defiance.

"Then you must come with me!" said Ivan. "Silver Wolf and I have come to take you home. Koshchey is sleeping. Let's go now while we have the chance."

Even as he spoke, the great door of the castle opened and a hundred hideous creatures spilled out, shrieking and howling.

"Koshchey never sleeps," roared a voice, and the sorcerer himself appeared.

Dressed in a long robe and scarlet cloak, he towered above them all. Ivan drew his sword and rushed at him, slashing at the demons that leaped to defend their master. Silver Wolf jumped from the shadows to help, snapping and snarling.

Koshchey laughed. "You can't kill me, little prince," he mocked. "I have hidden my soul outside my body. I am a thousand years old. I am Koshchey the Deathless!"

"Look in the old tree-stump!" Silver Wolf hissed at Ivan. "You'll find a box hidden there. Run!"

But before Ivan could move, Koshchey raised his arms. Ivan felt a terrible numbness in his legs.

The princess screamed. Ivan was turning to stone.

Chapter 5

The end of Koshchey

A gust of wind billowed under Prince Ivan's cloak. The Firebird's feather fluttered out, brushing his stony feet.

Warmth and feeling came back
to his legs. He spotted the tree
stump and raced over to it, while
Silver Wolf leaped at Koshchey's
face. Taken by surprise, the sorcerer
struggled to defend himself. His
creatures whirled helplessly around
the fighting pair, like dead leaves
in a December storm.

Meanwhile, Ivan reached
inside the tree stump and found
something hard-edged and heavy.
He pulled out an iron-bound box,
and opened it to find a gleaming
golden egg.

Koshchey suddenly saw what
the Prince had unearthed. His
shriek of horror filled the sky.

Ivan squeezed the egg, and
Koshchey doubled up in pain.
Then Ivan tossed the egg from one
hand to the other. Koshchey was
flung right across the garden,
and Silver Wolf fell to the ground.

"Don't destroy it!" Koshchey screamed. "Take whatever you want!"

But Ivan raised the egg high, and threw it to the ground where it smashed into pieces. A wisp of smoke rose from the fragments, and the sorcerer was gone.

For a moment, there was silence. Then Ivan and the princess heard a sound like ice cracking, and the murmuring of strange voices. All around the garden, the statues were coming back to life. They exclaimed in amazement, carefully stretching their stiff limbs.

Ivan rushed anxiously to where
Silver Wolf was lying, but the wise
old beast scrambled to his feet
unhurt. Then the air shivered. With
a great roar, the castle crashed and
crumbled to the ground.

When the dust cleared around the garden, Ivan was amazed to see no trace of the castle. Instead, there was a glittering city. He heard the sound of cheering, louder and louder, as the city folk rushed to welcome and thank him.

"We have been buried under Koshchey's castle for hundreds of years," they said. "You've set us free! Please stay and be our king."

But Ivan only wanted to take the princess home to her father, and to see his own father again. So they said their goodbyes and climbed onto Silver Wolf's back.

57

Chapter 6

Home at last

By evening, they could see the
lights of King Afron's palace.
The king was overjoyed to see his
daughter, and even happier to give
his blessing for her marriage to
Prince Ivan.

They celebrated the wedding
with a great feast, until even Silver
Wolf thought he could never be
hungry again.

King Afron rode the Horse of Power, and Ivan and the princess rode Silver Wolf, through the skies to King Dalmat's palace. There the two kings settled their quarrel to wish Ivan and the princess well, and sent them on their way with the Firebird.

Ivan's father had given up all
hope of his son's return. Imagine
his joy to see Ivan, not only alive
and well, but happily married to a
beautiful wife.

And the Firebird?

"I was wrong," said the king. "No one should try to own a bird like that. I shall set her free. She may come to the orchard and eat my apples whenever she likes."

And so she did. Every time the Firebird visited the orchard, she took an apple and scattered the seeds somewhere else. In time, another apple tree would grow. The new trees never did produce golden fruit, but still the apples were the sweetest you ever tasted.

The Firebird is one of the best-known and best-loved Russian folktales. One version of the story inspired a famous ballet, with music by Igor Stravinsky.

Designed by Michelle Lawrence
Series designer: Russell Punter
Series editor: Lesley Sims

Digital manipulation: Nick Wakeford

First published in 2010 by Usborne Publishing Ltd., Usborne House, 83-85 Saffron Hill, London EC1N 8RT, England. www.usborne.com
Copyright © 2010 Usborne Publishing Ltd.